'Saint' Merryn

---

*For Ray, William
and Johnny Dollar*

Since Dad Left copyright © Frances Lincoln Limited 1998
Text and illustrations copyright © Caroline Binch 1998

First published in the United States in 1998
by The Millbrook Press, Inc., 2 Old New Milford Road,
Brookfield, CT 06804.

First published in Great Britain in 1998
by Frances Lincoln Limited, 4 Torriano Mews,
Torriano Avenue, London NW5 2RZ.

Library of Congress Cataloging-in-Publication Data

Binch, Caroline.
Since Dad left / by Caroline Binch.
p.   cm.
Summary: Sid must learn to deal with his parents'
separation and the lifestyle his father has chosen.
ISBN 0-7613-0357-X (lib. bdg.)
ISBN 0-7613-0290-5 (trade)
[1. Parent and child—Fiction. 2. Separation
(Psychology)—Fiction.]   I. Title.
PZ7.B5116S1   1998
[E]—dc21

                              96-97644
                                 CIP
                                 AC

Printed in Hong Kong

5 4 3 2 1

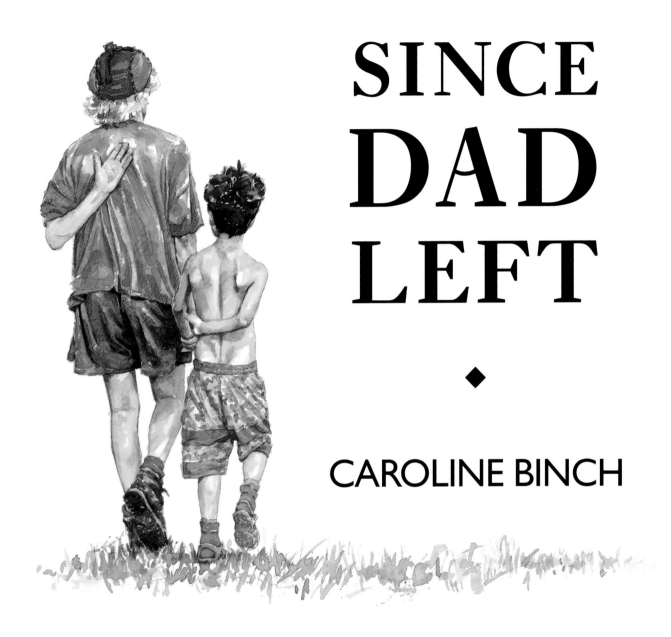

SINCE
DAD
LEFT

◆

CAROLINE BINCH

The Millbrook Press
Brookfield, Connecticut

Sid was angry. He often felt angry, now that his Mum and Dad didn't live together anymore.

He still had Doggo and Digger, of course, plus the three cats, Marmite, Bertha, and Kitty Mama. And most important of all—Mum.

"It just wasn't working out with Dad and me together," said Mum. "We were both unhappy."

Sid didn't understand. He thought they were more unhappy now.

Most days, Sid had school to think about. He liked to get up early in the morning and eat a big bowl of cereal in the kitchen. Then he and Mum walked down the path to wait for the school bus.

His friends caught the same bus and there was always lots to talk about. But since Dad left, there were times when he just wanted to sit by himself and look out the window.

At school, Sid liked art best of all.
He loved to paint skies filled with
rockets and moons and stars.
His teacher said he was
very good at rockets.

"Someday, I'm going to rocket into space and find a new planet," Sid told his friends. They all wanted to come with him, but Sid knew there wouldn't be enough food and oxygen for everyone—just enough for him, Mum and Dad, Doggo and Digger, and the cats.

After school, the bus brought Sid home and he ate his snack on the sofa watching television.

Since Dad left, Doggo and Digger were allowed to snuggle up with him.

Sometimes, Josh and Ben came to play. Their favorite game was hide-and-seek because Sid's house had lots of good places to hide. Now, Sid sometimes stayed lost even after the game was over. He liked being tucked away in a secret place where no one could find him.

One Saturday, Sid was extra cross. He stepped on Doggo's tail and didn't care when the dog yelped.

"I don't want to see Mick," said Sid angrily. "I don't like him. He went away."

"He's your dad, Sid. And it's only for one day," said Mum. "He misses you a lot. It isn't all his fault."

"He's not my dad anymore," said Sid, scowling, "and I don't want to go."

But Mum insisted. She drove Sid the few miles to where Mick was living, near Grandad's house.

When he saw Mick, Sid didn't know what to do.
He decided not to say a word. Mum and Mick
didn't speak to each other, so why should he?

Mick didn't seem to notice that Sid wasn't talking,
or that he had on his fiercest "hate you" face.

"It's great to see you, Sid. I've thought of lots of
things for us to do," said Mick. He patted and fussed
over the dogs, who were overjoyed to see him.

"Traitors," thought Sid. Dogs swapped sides
far too easily.

"I've just got to milk the goats, Sid, and then I'll
show you what I've been doing since I last saw you."

Sid was dying to say, "I don't care," in his
nastiest voice. He sat down and pretended
not to see or hear Mick, the goats,
or those stupid dogs.

"I'll just tie up the goats so they don't wander off and get into mischief," said Mick. "Then you can see my new house."

"That's not a house – you can't live there!" The words jumped out of Sid's mouth before he could stop them.

"Oh, it may look strange," said Mick, smiling. "But it's better than most houses, I can tell you. Come and see."

Sid followed Mick inside. He saw a wood-burning stove, a cooker, a big bed, and a little bed.

"Try the bed," said Mick.
Sid tried it, reluctantly.

"It's hard. I'm not sleeping here, ever," said Sid. He jumped down and walked outside. He was so surprised by Mick's new home, he'd forgotten that he wasn't speaking to him.

"Well, anytime you change your mind, I'd love you to stay," said Mick. "Doggo and Digger seem to like it."

Mick picked up a backpack.

"I've got some bread and cheese in here, so we can go for a ride with Oliver and the cart," he said.

Mick had been promising to fix up the cart for as long as Sid could remember. Now there it was, newly painted in bright colors.

While Mick was harnessing Oliver to the cart, Sid gave the horse some carrots. He loved how Oliver's big, soft, bristly mouth trembled against his hand.

He had been missing Oliver a lot.

Out on the narrow lanes, Oliver's hooves clip-clopped,
his big tail swished at flies, and his ears twitched. Sid started
to feel better. If only Mum could be here, too!

It was hot. Mick took Oliver through an old gate and into the woods, where the trail stopped by a lake.

"Well, I'm going for a swim," said Mick. "You coming, Sid?"

Sid felt silly sitting in the cart while Oliver munched grass and Mick and the dogs enjoyed the water.

He stepped carefully through the squishy mud at the edge of the lake.

It felt so good in the water
that Sid forgot to be angry.
It was just like old times.

Late in the afternoon when they got back, Mick put Oliver in the field and fed the dogs. Then he started making supper. Sid was tired. He climbed up into a tree where he could watch Mick.

"I'd love you to stay
and sleep over tonight,
Sid," said Mick, "but if
you want to go home,
that's fine. Some friends
are coming later, so I'm
lighting a fire."
Sid didn't answer.
He wanted to stay—but
he wanted to go home.

Mick's friends arrived laughing and talking. They sat around the fire, eating under the stars. One of them, Sean, told ghost stories especially for Sid. They played music on drums, a trumpet, and long didgeridoos, which made funny burpy sounds and made Sid laugh. They sang, too—fast songs that they all clapped to, then some soft songs that made Sid feel sad. Mum had a beautiful voice, but she hadn't sung since Dad left.

Sid sighed, and fell asleep between Mick, Doggo, and Digger. The last thing he remembered was Mick tucking him into bed.

"I'll stay tonight, Dad," he said sleepily.

Mick kissed his forehead. "I'm very happy to have you here. Sleep tight."

The singing and laughing outside warmed Sid's dreams.

Next morning, when Sid woke up, he went outside and found Mick having a cup of tea.

"Hi, Sid," said Mick. "Want some breakfast?"

Sid said nothing. He didn't want Mick to think everything was okay.

Mick came and sat by him with a cup of milk. "Look, Sid, I feel really bad about Mum, and breaking up and hurting you. But we both love you. And I miss you. It would be good if you could come again next weekend. See how you feel later on."

Sid wanted to hit Mick as hard as he could—but give him a big hug at the same time.

Then he saw Mum, and ran off across the field shouting to her. It must have been the wind that made his eyes water.

"Hello, my wonderful boy," said Mum. "I'm so happy to see you." Her smile made him feel like smiling, too. He looked back and saw Mick still watching.

"Bye, Dad," he shouted. "See you soon."